A FAMILY is a FAMILY is a FAMILY

Written by
Sara O'Leary

Illustrated by
Qin Leng

GROUNDWOOD BOOKS
HOUSE OF ANANSI PRESS
TORONTO   BERKELEY

WE WERE TALKING about families at school.
　　The teacher asked us what we thought made our
family special.

I went last because I wasn't sure what to say. My family is not like everybody else's.

"My mom and dad have been best friends since first grade. They really like each other. It's kind of gross."

"There are lots of kids in our family.
Mom and Dad just keep coming home
with more."

"Both my moms are terrible singers.
And they both like to sing really loud."

"I have more grandparents
than anybody else I know."

"We have a new baby in our house.
I think my mom ordered him online."

"We all look alike in my family. We just kind of go together."

"One week Mom gets me. The next week Dad does. Fair's fair."

"Some people say I look like my dad and some people say I look like my mom. I think I look like myself."

"My mom says that before I was
born I grew in her heart."

"Because I live with my grandmother, people sometimes think she's my mother. She's not. She's my everything."

"Some of the kids were Dad's when he met Mom. Some were Mom's when she met Dad. Now we all belong to each other."

"One of my dads is tall and one is short. They both give good hugs."

I listened to everybody else, and then
I remembered the time someone saw us
all together at the park.

She asked my foster mother to point
out her real children.

"Oh, I don't have any imaginary
children," Mom said. "All my children
are real."

A family ... is

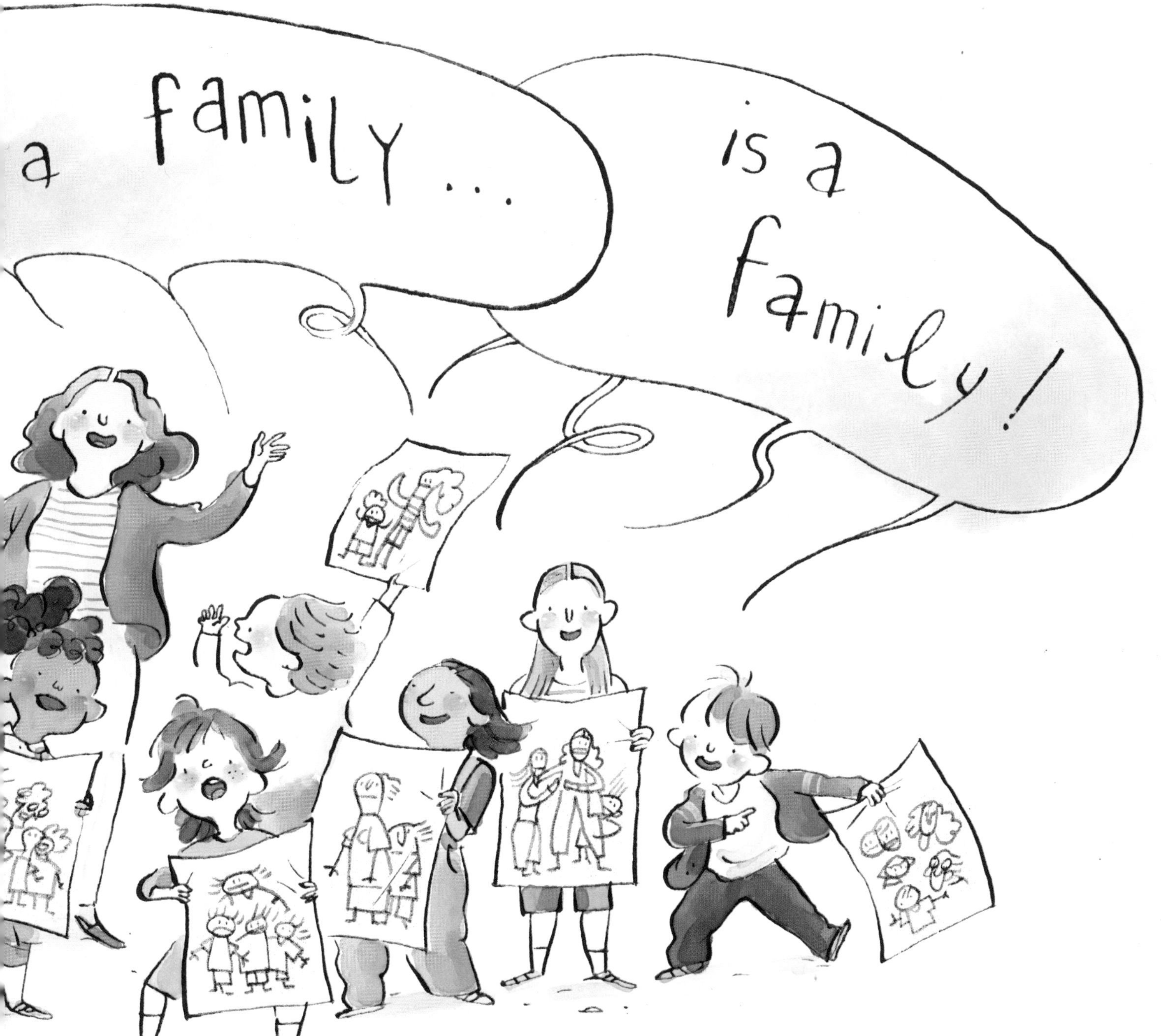
a family ...
is a family!

For Euan O'Leary, for telling me this is a good book. — S.O'L.

•

To Mom, Dad, Sansan … thank you for being the very best family and for giving me thirty-two years of pure happiness, with many more to come!

Special thanks to Mark, who I love more than anything and who has been a great source of inspiration with this book. — Q.L.

Text copyright © 2016 Sara O'Leary
Illustrations copyright © 2016 Qin Leng

Published in 2016 by Groundwood Books / House of Anansi Press
groundwoodbooks.com
Tenth printing 2021

Groundwood Books respectfully acknowledges that the land on which we operate is the Traditional Territory of many Nations, including the Anishinabeg, the Wendat and the Haudenosaunee. It is also the Treaty Lands of the Mississaugas of the Credit.

We gratefully acknowledge for their financial support of our publishing program the Canada Council for the Arts, the Ontario Arts Council and the Government of Canada.

Library and Archives Canada Cataloguing in Publication
O'Leary, Sara, author
A family is a family is a family / Sara O'Leary ; pictures by Qin Leng.
Issued in print and electronic formats.
ISBN 978-1-55498-794-8 (hardcover). — ISBN 978-1-55498-795-5 (pdf)
1. Families — Juvenile fiction. I. Leng, Qin, illustrator II. Title.
PS8579.L293F34 2016   jC813'.54   C2015-908421-0
                                                 C2015-908422-9

The illustrations were done in ink on paper and digital painting.
Design by Michael Solomon
Printed and bound in Canada

MIX
Paper from responsible sources
FSC® C016245

Canada Council
for the Arts
Conseil des Arts
du Canada

ONTARIO ARTS COUNCIL
CONSEIL DES ARTS DE L'ONTARIO
an Ontario government agency
un organisme du gouvernement de l'Ontario

With the participation of the Government of Canada
Avec la participation du gouvernement du Canada | Canada